WITHDRAWN

HOW BANKS WORK

Gillian Houghton

PowerKiDS
press™

New York

Published in 2009 by The Rosen Publishing Group, Inc.
29 East 21st Street, New York, NY 10010

First Edition

Editor: Joanne Randolph
Book Design: Julio Gil
Photo Researcher: Jessica Gerweck

Photo Credits: Cover © Elente Production/Age Fotostock; back cover, p. 18 Shutterstock.com; p. 5 © www.istockphoto.com; p. 6 © Merten/Age Fotostock; p. 9 © Jeffrey Smith/ www.istockphoto.com; p. 10 © Jim Cummins/Getty Images; p. 13 © David Lees/Getty Images; p. 14 © SuperStock/Age Fotostock; p. 17 © Dennie Cody/Getty Images; p. 21 © Luis Sierra/ www.istockphoto.com.

Library of Congress Cataloging-in-Publication Data

Houghton, Gillian.
  How banks work / Gillian Houghton. — 1st ed.
     p. cm. — (Invest kids)
  Includes index.
  ISBN 978-1-4358-2770-7 (library binding) — ISBN 978-1-4358-3205-3 (pbk.)
ISBN 978-1-4358-3211-4 (6-pack)
  1. Banks and banking–Juvenile literature. I. Title.
  HG1609.H68 2009
  332.1—dc22
                                                    2008035166

Manufactured in the United States of America

Contents

What Is a Bank?

Do you keep your money in a special place, such as a piggy bank, a dresser drawer, or a shoe box? You might want to keep it someplace very safe where it can grow! You might want to keep your money in a bank. A bank is a kind of business.

Banks take care of money for their customers, or the people and businesses that use the bank. Banks also give **loans** of money to their customers. This means they will let customers borrow money and pay it back later. Most banks also change one kind of currency, or paper money, for another.

There are thousands of banks in the United States. Some of them are large and some are small, but they all take care of money for their customers.

This is the inside of a commercial bank, which helps people take care of their money. People can save and borrow money at a commercial bank.

Kinds of Banks

One kind of bank is a commercial bank. Commercial banks help people, businesses, and governments save and borrow money. Personal bankers work mostly with people, such as you and your family, helping them save their money. Business bankers serve small businesses, such as a family-owned shoe store.

Thrift banks, such as **credit unions**, are run by people in a neighborhood and are not-for-profit. They help people and businesses that do not have the money to use commercial banks.

Investment banks work with corporations, or very large businesses. They help these corporations do business with one another.

Who Works in a Bank?

Let's take a look at the inside of a bank. You will likely see a row of desks. That is where the personal bankers meet with customers. Personal bankers help customers open **savings accounts** and **checking accounts**, take out loans, and invest in other bank services.

You might also see a long counter, or desk. Bank tellers work behind the counter. Bank tellers help customers **deposit** and **withdraw** money, change currency, and pay bills.

Many other people work in the bank. Accountants keep track of all the money that goes in and out of the bank. The bank manager makes sure the bank is running well.

Bank workers help customers who want to open accounts, withdraw or deposit money, or take out loans with the bank. They make sure a customer's account is up-to-date.

This girl is opening up a savings account at a bank. The bank will use her money and pay her interest, which means her money will grow.

How Do Banks Make Money?

Now we know who works at the bank, but how do banks make money? The bank uses the money customers put into the bank to pay loans or make investments.

Banks pay customers **interest** on their savings so that these people will let banks use their money. The banks, in turn, charge the customers who need loans interest. The interest banks charge for loans is more than the interest banks pay to customers with savings accounts. That is how banks make money! They also make money from the investments they make in other companies.

What Is Interest?

Interest is extra money. Banks give interest to customers who keep money in savings accounts, and they ask for interest from customers who borrow money.

When you deposit money into a savings account, you agree to an interest rate, which is usually listed as a **percent**. This is the amount of money the bank will give you for every dollar you keep in your account. Most accounts offer **compound** interest. This means the bank figures out the interest based on what you first put in plus any interest that has been paid. If you let your money stay in the bank, it grows more each year!

Have a parent help you find out how much your bank pays in interest. Do the math together to find out how much your money will grow over five years in a savings account.

Money is kept in a big safe called a vault at the bank. Vaults make it hard for robbers to come to the bank and take other people's money or belongings.

Taking Care of Your Money

No one has to keep their money in the bank. Many people decide to do so. There are many reasons why people open bank accounts. One reason is that the bank pays you interest and uses your money to help other people and businesses. There is another big reason to keep your money in the bank. When your money is in the bank, it is safe.

The Federal Deposit Insurance Corporation, or the FDIC, cares for almost all banks. The government runs the FDIC. Its job is to make sure banks are following the rules and being careful with their customers' money. If a bank fails and loses their customers' savings, the FDIC pays back up to $100,000 of the money that each customer had in the bank.

Start Saving!

Before you open a savings account, you should learn a little about the banks in your neighborhood and the kinds of accounts each one offers. Ask questions.

For example, does the FDIC care for the bank? What is the interest rate for a savings account? Is interest compounded, and if so, how often? Does the bank charge you a **fee** every time you withdraw money? Do you have to keep a certain amount of money in the account at all times? Each bank is a little different. Asking questions will help you choose the one that is best for you.

You can start saving your money even before you open a savings account. Once you have enough set aside, you can open an account at the bank that works best for you.

When you give someone a check, you and your bank are promising to pay that person. You should always write a check using a pen so no one can change what you write.

Check, Please!

A checking account allows you to withdraw money in the form of a personal check. You will likely not have a checking account for a long time, but it is still important to understand how it works!

A personal check is a piece of paper made by a bank. To pay by check, you write the name of the **receiver** and the amount of money being paid, sign your name, and then give the check to the receiver. The receiver takes the check to his bank. His bank then asks your bank to withdraw money from your account. You need to make sure you have enough money in your bank account, or the bank will charge you a fee to cover the check.

Electronic Banking

Did you know that you can use your bank on the Internet, on the phone, and at an ATM machine? These are all examples of **electronic** banking.

"ATM" stands for "automated teller machine." These machines can be found in banks, in stores, and on the street. ATMs allow bank customers to deposit and withdraw money. To use an ATM, you need an ATM card, which is a small piece of plastic with a magnetic strip or a microchip on one side. When you put the card into the machine, the machine reads the magnetic strip, which includes facts about your accounts.

This is an ATM machine. When you put your card in, the machine sends an electronic message to your bank, which in turn withdraws or deposits money in your account.

Bank on It!

Banks have been around for thousands of years. The first banks were probably housed in temples, or holy places. Instead of money, early people traded grains, tools, and metals for goods. They stored these items in the temples to make sure they were safe. Banks have grown and changed since early times. They are still the safest place to keep your money, though.

Today, banks are larger and more powerful than ever before. American banks work with customers around the world. You could be one of them. Ask your parent or teacher to help you get started saving today!

GLOSSARY

checking accounts (CHEK-ing uh-KOWNTS) Special places where a bank keeps money set aside for a person, which can be taken out using a check.

compound (KOM-pownd) Two or more things put together.

credit unions (KREH-dit YOON-yunz) Places where a person can save and borrow money that are owned and run by their members.

deposit (dih-PAH-zut) To put into something.

electronic (ih-lek-TRAH-nik) Having to do with electricity and computers.

fee (FEE) Extra money you must pay.

interest (IN-ter-est) The extra cost that someone pays in order to borrow money or the extra money banks give to people with savings accounts.

investment (in-VEST-ment) Putting money into something, such as a company, in the hope of getting more money later on.

loans (LOHNZ) Money given to people that must be paid back later.

percent (pur-SENT) One part of 100.

receiver (rih-SEE-ver) The person who takes something.

savings accounts (SAYV-ingz uh-KOWNTS) Special places where a bank keeps money set aside for a person.

withdraw (with-DRAW) To take out of something.

INDEX

B
bankers, 7–8
bank tellers, 8
bills, 8
business(es), 4, 7

C
checking account(s), 8, 19
corporations, 7
credit unions, 7
currency, 4, 8
customer(s), 4, 8, 11–12, 15, 20, 22

D
desk(s), 8
drawer, 4

F
family, 7
fee, 16

G
government(s), 7, 15

I
interest, 11–12, 16
investments, 11

L
loan(s), 4, 8, 11

M
manager, 8

R
receiver, 19

S
savings, 11, 15
savings account(s), 8, 11–12, 16
store(s), 7, 20

WEB SITES

Due to the changing nature of Internet links, PowerKids Press has developed an online list of Web sites related to the subject of this book. This site is updated regularly. Please use this link to access the list:
www.powerkidslinks.com/ikids/banks/